by Sherry North illustrated by Marcellus Hall

BECAUSE I AM YOUR DADDY

Abrams Books for Young Readers, New York

The illustrations in this book
were created using watercolors on paper.

Library of Congress Cataloging-in-Publication Data

North, Sherry.
Because I am your daddy / by Sherry North ; illustrated by Marcellus Hall.
p. cm.
Summary: In illustrations and verse, lists some of the many ways a father,
whether pilot or baseball player, could show his love for his child.
ISBN 978-0-8109-8392-2
[1. Stories in rhyme. 2. Father and child—Fiction.]
I. Hall, Marcellus, ill. II. Title.

PZ8.3.N8135Be 2010
[E]—dc22
2009003063

Book design by Chad W. Beckerman

Published in 2010 by Abrams Books for Young Readers,
an imprint of ABRAMS. All rights reserved. No portion of this book may be
reproduced, stored in a retrieval system, or transmitted in any form or by any means,
mechanical, electronic, photocopying, recording, or otherwise, without
written permission from the publisher.

Printed and bound in China
10 9 8 7 6 5 4 3 2 1

Abrams Books for Young Readers are available at special discounts when purchased
in quantity for premiums and promotions as well as fundraising or educational use.
Special editions can also be created to specification. For details, contact
specialmarkets@abramsbooks.com or the address below.

ABRAMS
THE ART OF BOOKS SINCE 1949
115 West 18th Street
New York, NY 10011
www.abramsbooks.com

For Jonna
—S. N.

For Peter, Margaret, and Rachel
—M. H.

If I were a pilot, I would fly you to your school.

Your friends would all look up and say, "Your daddy is so cool!"

If I were a slugger, I would spot you in the stands

And swing my bat to hit the ball straight into your hands.

If I were a scientist, we would dig up ancient bones

And find the biggest dinosaur the world has ever known.

If I were a carpenter, I would use my saw and drill

To build two wooden go-karts for racing down the hill.

If I were a drummer, I would lead a marching band,

And you would ride my shoulders in parades across the land.

If I were a ranger, I would share my hideaway

So we could peek across the creek where wolf pups drink and play.

If I were a surfer, I would take you on my board

And ride a wall of water as it tumbles toward the shore.

If I were a director, I would cast you as my star.

Your face would light up movie screens in cities near and far.

If I were an explorer, I would guide you through dark caves.

Stalactites lined with glowworm lights would help us find our way.

If I were an inventor, I would make a high-tech tree

That pops open a tree house when you turn the secret key.

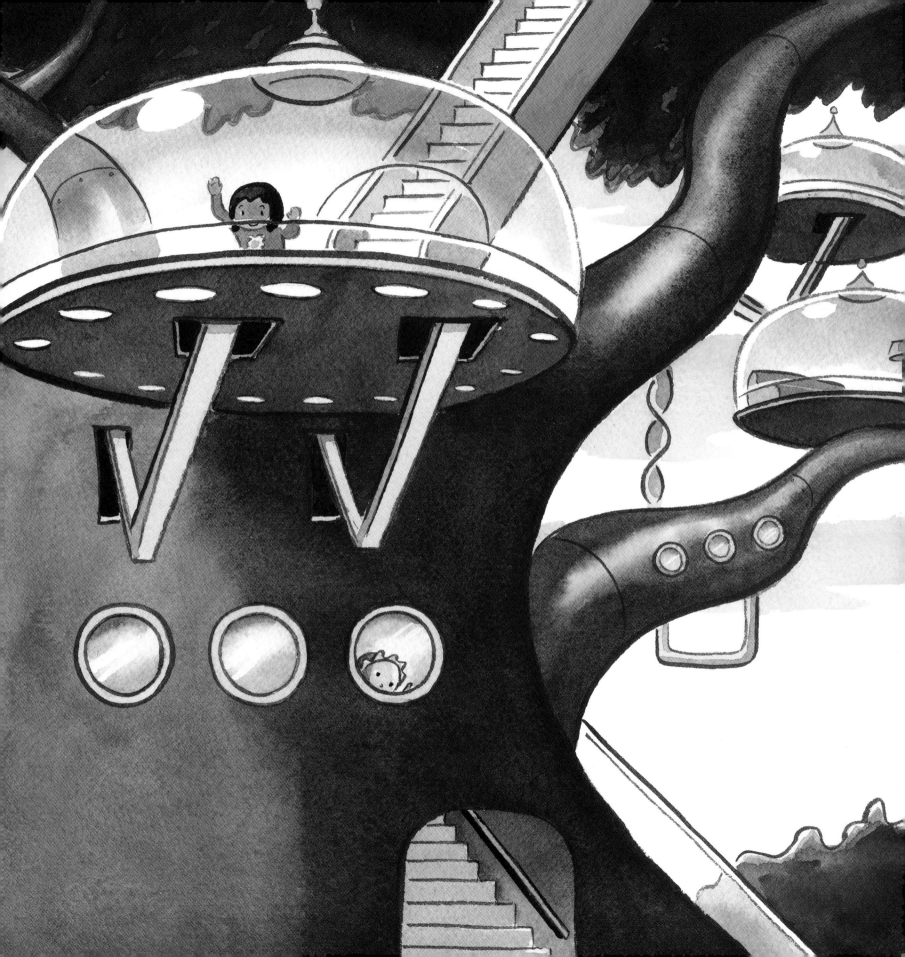

If I were a librarian, we could venture anywhere.

Wherever we decide to go, a book would take us there.

If I were a musher, we would glide on arctic snow

And gaze up as the northern lights put on their brilliant show.

If I were a Martian, then you would be one, too!

Our spaceship would have cosmic bowling and a robot crew.

And if I were a wizard, I would make your dreams come true . . .

Because I am your daddy, I would do anything for you.